STAR WARS ®

THE DARK LORD RISING: BOOK 1

Adapted by Benjamin Harper

studio **fun**

A READER'S DIGEST COMPANY

White Plains, New York • Montréal, Québec • Bath, United Kingdom

Young Anakin Skywalker lived on the desert planet Tatooine. He and his mother were slaves, and Anakin worked in a junk shop. One day, Jedi Knight Qui-Gon Jinn entered the shop. The Jedi were guardians of peace in the galaxy. Qui-Gon had been on a mission to Naboo, where he rescued Queen Amidala from a droid army that had seized control of her planet. The two had landed on Tatooine to find parts to repair their ship.

Qui-Gon recognized that Anakin was very powerful in the Force, an energy field that connected every living thing and gave Jedi their powers. Qui-Gon freed Anakin from slavery and took him away to train as a Jedi.

Queen Amidala was fighting to get Naboo back. Anakin piloted a craft and destroyed the starship controlling the droids. He saved the planet and proved to the Jedi Council that he was very strong in the Force. The leading Jedi allowed Obi-Wan Kenobi, Qui-Gon Jinn's former apprentice, to train Anakin after Qui-Gon was defeated in battle.

Ten years later, Anakin had become a powerful Jedi. He and Master Obi-Wan Kenobi fought valiantly in the Clone Wars—a galactic civil war that the Republic waged with troops of clones led by Jedi against the droid armies of the Confederacy of Independent Systems. But more and more, Anakin felt the Jedi Council was hiding information from him and not allowing him to use his full power.

Secretly, he had fallen in love with and married Padmé Amidala, now a Senator for the Republic. He began having terrible dreams about the future where Padmé died.

When Anakin discovered that the ruler of the Republic, Chancellor Palpatine, was a Sith Lord named Darth Sidious, the Chancellor asked him to become a Sith and help end the war. He claimed that their combined power in the Force could end the galactic conflict. Darth Sidious promised to help Anakin keep his nightmares from coming true—together, they could save Padmé and restore peace to the galaxy.

The Sith used the dark side of the Force to gain power and were the sworn enemies of the Jedi. But Anakin was desperate to save Padmé, and he turned to the dark side. Darth Sidious named his new apprentice Darth Vader. Vader's first task was to help wipe out the Jedi, whom Darth Sidious claimed were trying to take control of the galaxy.

7

Darth Sidious declared himself Emperor of the galaxy and took complete control of the government. He turned Darth Vader against his former master, Obi-Wan Kenobi. In a fateful duel, the onetime friends fought their way across the volcano planet Mustafar's molten surface until they found themselves battling on a floating platform racing above a lava river.

They fought with lightsabers, Jedi weapons that emitted beams of energy. Powerful in the Force, they were both equally matched in battle. Finally, Obi-Wan flipped off the platform onto the riverbank. Darth Vader attempted to jump as well, but Obi-Wan defeated him.

Darth Vader was terribly injured. The Emperor arrived on Mustafar to bring his apprentice back to Coruscant, the central planet of the galaxy, where medical droids fitted him with life-support armor. Darth Vader would need to wear the armor to stay alive. As the mask sealed over Darth Vader's face, it began to breathe for him. He was trapped in the armor that would make him feared across the galaxy.

On a faraway world called Polis Massa, Padmé had twins, Luke and Leia, but then she passed away. Obi-Wan Kenobi and Jedi Master Yoda separated the children, so that Darth Vader and the Emperor would have a hard time finding them. Leia was sent to the planet Alderaan, and Luke went to live on Tatooine.

Almost twenty years passed after Anakin turned to the dark side. Darth Vader now served the Emperor and was on a mission to crush the Rebellion, a small group fighting to gain control of the galaxy from the Emperor. On a giant Imperial ship called a Star Destroyer, he zoomed through space to capture Princess Leia. He suspected her of aiding rebel spies who had stolen blueprints to the Empire's Death Star, a massive space station that could destroy planets. The rebels intended to use the plans to destroy it. Vader needed to get the blueprints back.

　　High above Tatooine, Darth Vader finally caught
Princess Leia. Her ship was dragged into the Star Destroyer's
docking bay. Stormtroopers, soldiers of the Empire, raced into
the rebel ship and cleared the way for Darth Vader to enter.
He confronted the ship's captain—and then seized Princess Leia.
He couldn't find the stolen plans, but he took Leia prisoner and
vowed to make her tell him where she had hidden them.

Leia was taken to the detention center on the Death Star. She was startled when her cell door opened and Darth Vader entered, along with an interrogator droid. "And now, your highness, we will discuss the location of your hidden rebel base,"  the Dark Lord rasped as the door slammed shut and the droid approached her with a truth serum.

Later, Darth Vader argued with Imperial Admiral Motti. He had been unsuccessful obtaining information from Princess Leia. Admiral Motti mocked Darth Vader about his inability to use the Force to uncover any information.

"Your sad devotion to that ancient religion has not helped you conjure up the stolen data tapes," Admiral Motti scoffed, angering Lord Vader, who used the Force to choke the Imperial officer. "I find your lack of faith disturbing," the Sith Lord said before releasing Motti from his grip.

Darth Vader sensed a disturbance in the Force. Obi-Wan Kenobi and young Luke Skywalker, whom he was training as a Jedi, had commissioned pilot Han Solo and Wookiee copilot Chewbacca to take them to Alderaan aboard the *Millennium Falcon* to deliver the stolen Death Star plans to rebel leaders.

But the ship was caught in the Death Star's tractor beam when it traveled too close to the space station. Luke, Han, and Chewbacca rescued Princess Leia while Obi-Wan deactivated the tractor beam so they could escape. But Obi-Wan's mission was not complete—he had to battle his former apprentice.

The two dueled with lightsabers. "Your powers are weak, old man," Darth Vader said. 🔲 "You can't win, Darth," Obi-Wan replied. "If you strike me down, I shall become more powerful than you can possibly imagine." Darth Vader then struck Obi-Wan with his lightsaber and the Jedi Knight disappeared.

The rebels escaped the Death Star and took the stolen data tapes with them. They analyzed the plans and found a weakness— and the time to strike was now!

But Darth Vader had placed a homing beacon on the *Millennium Falcon* before it blasted away from the Death Star so the Empire could trace the rebels to their hidden base. The deadly space station was on its way to Yavin 4, the planet where the rebels had built their base, to destroy the planet along with the Rebellion.

The rebels launched their attack.
Darth Vader realized the danger and decided
to take them on himself. He flew his starship
into battle and destroyed many rebels who were
attempting to destroy the Death Star.

21

One rebel pilot, Luke Skywalker, remained. He raced to complete his mission, with Darth Vader on his heels. "The Force is strong with this one," Darth Vader noted as he zeroed in on the rebel's X-wing starfighter.

Just as Vader prepared to fire on Luke, Han Solo flew in from behind and shot at Darth Vader's wingman. The out-of-control ship hit Vader's craft, sending the Dark Lord spinning into space. Luke fired his photon torpedo and destroyed the Death Star. As Darth Vader flew off, he vowed revenge against the young rebel.